# Introduction

Last time I wrote a book was in 2017. It was called *What Difference Does It Make? What Happened to Our Country,*[1] which happens to be a short, but accurate, encyclopedia of President Obama's activities to destroy this country, and it started with "I am elated."

Burt, my husband, confessed to me, "I feel happy…happy to sometimes live in this paradise called Florida, happy to be able to pursue my work [at age of eighty-one], and happy that we just dodged the final fatal bullet in the election and put Donald Trump in the White House." So Burt's well-being included three entities: a place, the ability to work, and the political environment.

It is all gone now, and I am left with nothing three years later. I hope you, the reader, will permit me to explain what had been and is no more. You will let me tell you about an individual that is so unique; people, including myself, often had doubts as to the veracity of it all, yet it was all true, without a shadow of a doubt, as I had found out the hard way—by getting solid proof.

Permit me to say one more thing: I am what a colleague of mine called a minimal writer—that is, I write only about facts, without embellishment and fancy descriptions, without back-and-forth conversations, an important feature of good writing, or without depiction of places to admire, which would give some relaxation. I write only about facts, which follow each other without pause.

I hope the reader will indulge me and not throw the book away in disgust, once he/she has made the endeavor to pick it up, because of too much concentrated effort. Just put the book down and continue after a good rest.

# 1

# A Fraudulent Election

It was the early morning of November 4th, 2020. All eyes were on the television and had been the whole night before. That morning, the result of the election was going to be announced. We were stunned and horrified at the result. My husband and I had happily noted all night as President Trump amassed votes. And suddenly, in the early morning, his votes were no longer counted, there was a complete stop, even on Fox News. What craziness was that?

We had gone to four of President Trump's rallies and saw most others on television. There were always thousands of people present, many of whom had to stay outside the meeting halls or enclosed areas. While Mr. Biden's "rallies," which were few and far between, had a maximum of one hundred or so attendants, most less than that. In fact, some had no more than fifteen attendees. It had been a joke going around that Mr. Biden was mostly hiding in the basement of his home.

How could this possibly be? How could Biden have won more votes than Mrs. Clinton when President Trump had done so well for this country and for all its citizens?

He had done wonders and even had accomplished most of the promises he had made during his run for the presidency. It was as if he was a magician. Much of what he accomplished were things that could never have been done nor even thought of by any other person. We, the conservative Republican citizens, all had concluded that President Trump was the best president of our lifetime, if not best President ever, the best and most appropriate to follow on the time of woe we had endured for the previous eight years.

Our economy was booming. He eliminated ISIS and, thus, made the country safe in a matter of a few weeks, which seemed could never happen again after these Islamic terrorists were in the process of building a caliphate over the Middle East and Africa under Obama. President Trump made the country independent of foreign gas and oil by increasing production of fossil fuel here in the USA, ensuring that it was done in a clean, environmentally friendly way, an incredible accomplishment in a short time, and reopening coal mining, thus also returning jobs to people who had lost them under the previous administration's war on coal. There were more jobs for all minorities whose job numbers never had increased before. He got rid of the Paris Accords (the global warming fantasy, which democrats declared our nation's worst problem) because we were paying the bulk of the money while other countries, who did the most pollution, paid nothing. President Trump got rid of laws that prevented businesses from thriving. He improved schools for minorities and everyone else by instituting school choice, and he improved minority universities by augmenting the money they received as subsidy from the federal government.

President Trump increased the number of the military, which had been depleted by the previous administration and gave them equipment they sorely needed. He infinitely improved veterans' lives by allowing them when sick to go to private doctors instead of hanging on for weeks and months to be seen, where often it was too late, and they die while waiting to be treated. He fired people who worked for the veterans' administration, collected their salary, but did nothing for or mistreated veterans.

President Trump established the Space Force to keep us safe from foreign powers and instituted ways to protect us from cyberattacks.

President Trump instituted the "Right to Try" that is letting people, who had diseases that did not improve after all conventional means, try new promising drugs not yet gone through the hoops to obtain the final stamp of approval by the CDC, the Center of Disease Control and the FDA, Food and Drug Administration.

Most importantly, President Trump started and continued to build a wall on our southern border and made arrangements with the Mexican government to help reduce the constant flood of illegals coming into our country, which resulted in the import of illicit drugs poisoning our children and teens; the free entrance of criminals and violent gangs; the reintroduction of diseases we had eradicated for years and had no medicines for like tuberculosis, measles, and whooping cough; the trafficking of women and children; and the overwhelming of our schools, hospitals, living quarters, and welfare system.

President Trump officially moved the American Embassy of Israel from Tel Aviv to Jerusalem, a thing that was promised but never accomplished. In addition, President Trump, with the help of his son-in-law Jared Kushner, created a miracle in the Middle East by making peace and furthering trade between some Arab nations and Israel, something unheard of. He managed to make peace between Israel and Egypt, Jordan, the United Arab Emirates, Bahrain, Morocco, Sudan. He called it appropriately the Abraham Accords. The President was able to get Iran to reduce its quest to produce atomic bombs by withdrawing from the nuclear deal instituted by his predecessor and by imposing many sanctions. Each one of these accomplishments would never have been done or even thought of if not for President Trump's unwavering love for this country and its people, his acumen, and high intelligence, his unbelievable stamina he had to work twenty hours a day, seven days a week. He did all that without taking a salary, donating it instead to a different charity each month.

All that was done while the democrats went after him with a vengeance that never let up. They called him a Russian Agent (a most inane, insane thing, as inane as maybe to say, way back then, that George Washington was working for the British). The democrats wanted to impeach him as soon as he got elected, even before he set foot in the White House. They wanted to impeach him for "Russia, Russia, Russia" (a song they sang to implicate him in illicit dealings with Russia, which were actually done by the very same people who accused him of it, but that is for another time and place) or for making an innocent call to the Ukraine, congratulating its leader for having been elected.

When COVID-19 broke out (a virus originating in a Chinese lab, which was heavily financed by democratic scientists from Harvard such as Professor Peter Berman and the National Institute of Health [NIH] under Professor Doctor Anthony Fauci), President Trump enacted another miracle. He brought people from industry and scientists together to produce three vaccines in a matter of months instead of years it usually took to make a vaccine (see Dr. Fauci's promise of an AIDS vaccine forty years ago, which still is nonexistent).

Mrs. Pelosi had predicted early on, before the 2020 elections, that the democrats had a feather in their cap (she said something about having arrows in her quiver) regarding the election, and sure enough with all the good things President Trump did to make this country safer, economically better, independent of foreign energy, great again, admired by foreign powers, in other words, "making America number 1 again," Mr. Biden won the election. He had been in the government for forty-eight years accomplishing nothing but becoming wealthy and making his entire family wealthy, yet he won the election, decided by the Democrats, who were helped by the media and some evil power, which had settled over our country. The Grand Old Party, GOP, called it the swamp, but it could be called the devil himself.

It was November 4th, 2020. Biden won the election, and I nagged my husband to get my passport renewed as it had run out. I wanted to leave the country. No way could I stay under democratic control. I did not have a single democratic acquaintance or relative I did not despise. They were of a different makeup than I. Lying and cheating, hating, envy, and unhappiness were their basic characteristics. They were never satisfied, always wanting more. They lived by words—words of idealism, "peace for all, plenty of money for all" is the idealism they were convinced, made them superior, these lofty thoughts, just thoughts, *they never moved a finger for*. Doing good for others, integrity, friendliness, common sense, ethics and morals, working hard to achieve one's goals (dreams) and doing well at whatever they were doing, following the rule of law, and abiding by the constitution was unknown to them. And so, I knew the America I loved with all my heart would disappear.[2]

Burt sat at his computer and wrote the letter needed to renew my passport, and as he finished and had to bend down to pick up a sheet of paper, which nefariously had fallen on the floor, his chair with its four wheels, rolled backward and he fell on the floor. He could not get up on his own, he had broken a hip. It was the 4th of November 2020 and the beginning of the end of our lives.

Burt was taken by ambulance to the Naples Hospital (NCH, Naples Community Hospital) and, the next day, was operated on under general anesthesia for a total hip replacement. My daughter and I were allowed to see him from 9:00 a.m. to 8 p.m., but the first day, we went there, eager to see him. Burt did not recognize us and had little seizures all over his body. We were in total agony till the nurse told us, reluctantly, that it was from the medication they had given him to ease his pain. He must have been allergic to it, and he would be better next day. I remained in agony and could not forgive myself for having caused him to fall. The next day, he was better, and I sat with him from nine to eight at night, every day, to make sure he did not get that medicine again and to encourage him and watch over him. He recuperated very slowly. Finally, he was able to benefit from physical therapy in the hospital and get in a condition to come home. He was so happy to be home; so grateful to be able to sleep without the other patient he had been saddled with in his room, who coughed and moaned all night. He continued the physical therapy three times a week at home till he was able to come off the wheel chair he had to use in the house and ambulate with a walker.

Not long thereafter, he came down with a fever of 104 degrees and had to go back by ambulance to the hospital because he had contracted COVID-19. I was only allowed to visit him there for two hours in the evening. After being medicated with three doses of "regeneron" he actually had to ask for to be given, as our Rabbi's wife counseled us, he felt better, and against my better judgment, having read that one had to get at least five doses of that Regeneron medication to benefit from it, the hospital sent him home. Again, he was delighted to be home, in his own bed, and told me very often how much he loved me and that I was everything to him. I was not comprehending his need to tell me that so frequently as our marriage was almost in its sixtieth year, and we had loved each other for all that time. It scared me to hear him say that so often, but I did not complain.

A few days later, I caught COVID-19 myself, which expressed itself not by high fever or any other symptom but an unbelievable weakness. One morning soon after he came home, he asked me to make breakfast for him, so I got up and, instead of going into the kitchen directly to make him some breakfast, I went to brush my teeth, and as I turned toward the kitchen, I fell and broke my left hip. Burt took one look at me, a desperate horrified look I will never forget, and called the ambulance to take me to Lee Memorial Hospital. I was oblivious to the fact that I was leaving Burt all alone and that he had not even had breakfast yet.

That same day, Burt must have given up his fight to live. He could not bear the fact that he was unable to watch over me as he had done in all the time we were together. He called our son-in-law, Michael, in New Jersey to please come to help him. Michael took the next plane and arrived at our house, but Burt could not get up to open the door. Michael found a window in the back of the house that I had left open, luckily, and he broke the screen in front of it, crawled through, and got into our house. He made Burt some food but had to feed it to him, Burt was so weak. Toward the evening, he got a high fever, so Michael called the ambulance to get him to the hospital again. The EMT people, however, would not take him to the hospital I was in, a last nail in his coffin. He became sicker and sicker and had to be intubated while all his vital organs failed him.

I could not go to be with him, it was not allowed, and I was unable to walk. On the last day of his life, my daughter decided on her own to ask the nurses in the ICU where he had been under an induced coma to wake him up to let me say goodbye on the iPhone. She meant well, but it was never my idea, and I would never have agreed to that. So I saw him on the iPhone looking horribly frightened and half crazed. Shortly thereafter, his heart gave out, and he passed away. I was left with the terrible memory of his beloved and beautiful face all distorted and far away.

That day, I lost it all, my best friend and protector, my solace, the one who kept me happy for some sixty-five years, my love, my life.

# 2

## Looking Back

It was going to be a milestone year, a year of celebration. Burt was having his eighty-fifth birthday, and we were going to have our sixtieth anniversary. We were intending to celebrate those milestones and had mulled over plans for them. For his birthday, we were going to be together with all our friends in his favorite restaurant. And this time, we were going to have the anniversary videotaped. On our twenty-fifth anniversary, the only other time we had treated ourselves with a real celebration, we had not taped it, and we were sorry not having that done because it turned out to be a wonderful party, with many of our friends and colleagues making unexpected complimentary speeches about our work and our togetherness. Our daughter had also composed a song to the tune of "My Favorite Things" from the *Sound of Music*, she sang to us. It was replete with interesting allusions to the work we were doing. She had absorbed much of our dinner conversations by then, had spent her summers doing science projects and had become familiar with the terminology.

We now had been together for sixty years not only living but working together for all that time. Even after I retired from active work, we hardly ever were apart. Burt was writing his many papers at home and going into the lab only every few days, for a day. He trusted his postdoctoral fellows to do the work he proposed and checked on them periodically but only briefly.

Burt, after his birthday, intended to write two more papers on different topics of our work, and then he had decided that we were going to write a book together. In April, despite just recuperating from the broken hip, he had finished the one paper and gotten it accepted in a good journal of his choosing, and he was putting the end touches on the other article. His incredible memory allowed him to write papers on work we had done years ago, sitting in the deep freeze, as I called it. But to him, it was as if we had completed it yesterday.

I was eager to start on the book. There was much I could not remember, but there would be no worries about that on my part. Burt, like for everything else, would remember and fill in the blanks.

I now have only a small bit of help to write this book. On the occasion of his eightieth birthday, he was asked to write a summary of his life for the *Journal of Physiology*, and so I have some very abbreviated material from that summary, which was never published because the people in charge thought it was too good to be true—plus my remembrances of our sixty years together, a smidgen of what Burt could have written. I am so infinitely lost and so very sad that all that time went by, and I could not hold on to it, could not hold on to him.

I will attempt to write this biographical sketch because it needs to be written to honor him, to keep a record of a man who was unique in every way. I will go back and forth between my memories of him, the things he told me about, and his own words from the summary for the *Journal of Physiology*.

# 3

# Childhood

Burt's parents and 2 brothers, when I first met them.

Burt adored his mother. He often told me how much his mother had made him into the person he was, and how much she had contributed to his abilities and endeavors and strength of character. Burt was the firstborn of three boys, but he had his mother all to himself for five wonderful years. He was so grateful for that. His memory of those years were warm, pleasant, and very clear. What stood out in his mind was going to the Brooklyn library by trolley, a treasure trove for him. After admiring the books, his mom let him choose four to six each time to take home to look at the pictures while she would read them to him. Eventually, he got to read them himself. She also took him to the Brooklyn Botanic Garden where they wandered around the many paths to admire the foliage, different trees, and various flowers, which made him appreciate and love those outings, too, and were the beginning of his fondness of the great outdoors.

His parents were not well-to-do. His father had a hard time making a living. He had devoted himself to helping one of his brothers who had suffered from rheumatic fever as a child. This left him weak and resulted in a stroke at the age of thirty-five, confining him to a wheelchair though his mind was all there. Burt's father felt compelled to work in the men's store, their father had left them to help him out and be there for him. The store had been a good business, but as time went on, competition appeared in the form of several other men stores, which caused financial disaster, no matter how many hours the store stayed open and how late his father came home.

But let me tell it in Burt's own words as he described his childhood on the occasion of his eightieth birthday, answering the *Journal of Physiology's* invitation for a summary of his life. He titled his response to Dr. Peter K. Lauf, the professor who sent him the invitation, "Today I Am the Luckiest Man on Earth"—quoting Lou Gehrig's final words on his retirement in 1939.

So far, it has been a wonderful and blessed life to be able to accomplish many of the things that the Lord brought me here to do. Why, you may ask, do I say "blessed life"? Coming from a poor family and my dad away from me for most of the day until I left home, I missed many of the wonderful things fathers do with their kids. But my fantastic, well-read mother would take me on the trolley in Brooklyn, where we lived, to the

New York Public Library, and we would borrow books from the time I was four years old on a variety of exciting subjects. At the beginning, it was children's books she read to me, but as soon as I could read, I tended to use the library for reference. If I wanted to understand something or learn something new, there was always the NYC library, my godsend.

During that time besides much reading, two other things attracted me: playing baseball and building model ships, trains, and airplanes. I would spend hours fine-tuning my pitching skills to where I developed seven different pitches. Pitching against my peers, I could strike out many batters each game. I got so much confidence in my playing that I thought, eventually, I should look for a major league contract, having bettered Bob Feller's fast ball with the Cleveland Indians and related to my friends that I could eventually break Christy Mathewson's record of 373 wins if given a chance. When several scouts eventually saw my skills, they did offer me a contract in the minor leagues. Being an upstart, I told them either they offer me a major league trial or there would be no deal. So it turned out to be no deal.

His mom saved every week from her food allowance to provide Burt the wherewithall to his other loves, constructing ships, trains, and airplanes from little pieces he glued together, following carefully all the directions from some manuals or books he had taken out on his library trips. He could spend days, he told me, sitting in his room, perfecting these delicate constructions. And when they were done, he could play with them, as the trains would move and the airplanes could fly.

As a result of his reading, Burt became fascinated with science at an early age.

> I then pestered my mom to buy me a chemistry set, which she saved up to finally obtain. I started spending my time experimenting with various chemicals. There came a time when one of the reactions produced a small explosion. Two things impressed me then: (1) what actually caused this explosive event and (2) how lucky I and my mother were, not to have gotten injured. At that moment I thanked God who saved us from a serious injury. The lesson I got out of that experience stayed with me: remember to be careful and prepare yourself properly beforehand when entering an unknown world!

Burt's mother guided him also to some books she had in her own library, one of which became his favorite: *Microbe Hunters* by Paul de Kruif. His interest in science became settled more firmly in his mind after perusing this and several other books like the novel written by A. J. Cronin: *The Citadel*, which talks about black-lung disease, among other things.

> Having now read and reread several of these books, I made up my mind to either become a research scientist or a physician-scientist. At age twelve, my mind was set on one of these two professions. However, I knew either one of these pathways would be difficult and costly in different ways. I also knew if and when I would be ready for college, my parents could not support any of the tuition. But since the age of seven, my dad had given me one very important piece of advice: "get a job, at least a part-time job."

So at age seven, Burt got a newspaper route. His father would take him on early in the morning, and he would place, not throw, the newspapers on the porch or in the driveway of his customers every weekday morning. And on weekends, his father would take him to get paid.

His father impressed on him during these trips the advice that to be successful in this world, you have to work, and work hard.

> After my first job of delivering newspapers, I have continued to work ever since up to the present time. Lucky me having this credo, I was able to "work my way through college."

His father was great to have around the house when he was home. He had a natural ability to repair things. He could pull things apart, fix whatever was defective, and put them together again, so they would work. He could do the same to cars and anything that needed fixing.

When the US entered WWII, Burt's father volunteered to work in the Brooklyn Navy Yard to help build the ships that were needed for the war effort. He became so efficient at it that he was asked to be the foreman of a group of workers building the USS *Iowa*. That position required his father to stay on the ship all week, coming home only one day of the weekend so Burt and his mom would only see him one day a week. However, he was well paid from the navy, and that was the only time the family was financially comfortable. He made good friends on the navy ships, and when the war was over, one of those friends asked him to come into business with him. This friend was in the diamond business, and he taught Burt's father to cut diamonds, which he picked up easily and became a master at. This business was going to make Burt's family financially comfortable for good. But Burt's sick uncle was sitting in the wings, and so his father could not get himself to follow his friend and went instead back to helping his brother in the clothing store.

As mentioned before, Burt missed the company of his father, who stayed in that store late into the night while other fathers played ball with their children, took them places, and did other sundry things. Burt felt deprived of all this and so turned his love to his mother.

Many times, however, he told me about that one single glorious day when his father took him fishing. It was a sunny morning in Long Island, and his father rented a boat, and the two went to Long Island Sound, where the fish were plentiful. His father taught him how to put lures on a little hook and how to cast and be quite still. And to his amazement and joy, Burt caught fish after fish while his father did not come up with a single one. I can't count how many times Burt told me that story with joy in his face followed by sadness, for his father never took him fishing again. Later on, Burt liked to hear the song "Cats in the Cradle" written by Harry Chapin and wife. It reminded him so much of his relationship with his father. I thought it was so sad.

Burt, nevertheless, credited his father with the one important lesson, and that is, "if you want to make it in this world, you have to get a job and work hard."

He also credited his father for teaching him to be grateful to the Lord for the blessings he had been given and, especially, to stay true to his religion[2].

# 4

# School

When it was time to start first grade, Burt made friends quickly in his class because some of his classmates lived close to his home, and he had been acquainted with them before. There was Allan Koenigsberg (later named Woody Allen), another kid whose name escaped me, and a fourth whom the three called "fish face" for fun. The four were constantly talking in class while the teacher was teaching, but when the teacher called on Burt to ask him a question on the subject she was talking about, he usually knew the answer, a characteristic of his ability to multitask, which he retained throughout the years and I so admired in him.

It was not just that the four kids were constantly talking, but Allan was making them laugh a lot. He was a comedian already at that tender age. The result of all this talking and laughing in class and not "paying attention to the teacher" made the teacher call Burt's mother often. Burt's mother knew her son, and tired of her being called in all the time, she said at one point to the teacher, "If you make the lessons you teach more interesting, my son would pay attention." That was the last time the teacher called Burt's mother. The principal told his mother that Burt would never amount to anything, if he continued in this way, but his mother knew better. She often told her son, "You can do anything you set your mind to, and you can do it well." She was so right. Burt got his knowledge not from school but from reading incessantly almost anything he came across. His thirst for knowledge was inexhaustible, and lo and behold, he remembered it all. He had a photographic memory that hardly ever let him down.

Coming back to elementary school, at the end of the year, when these four kids were in fourth grade, they were all skipped to sixth grade. The same teacher who taught them in fourth grade was going to teach fifth that year, and she just had her fill of their antics. The parents were told that those four students were simply too smart to need fifth grade, and therefore, could skip to the sixth directly. The parents did not know any better and accepted this with great pride.

These four kids would play together after school too, and Burt remembered how many times Allan's mother would yell out the window, "Allan, come practice your clarinet," or "Allan, go to your music lesson," which the kids knew he both thoroughly hated to do. (Later, Woody Allen told his audience how much he loved to play the clarinet and made quite a bit of to-do about it, but it was his mother's insistence which ultimately gave him the ability to play the clarinet as his friends knew.)

## Hebrew School

Burt's parents could not afford to belong to a temple. The cost was too great having to pay a yearly fee plus part of the cost of the building itself. One of his uncles got him a private tutor to teach him to read Hebrew and the prayers and readings you had to do for a *bar mitzvah* (a ritual thirteen-year-old Jewish boys go through to celebrate becoming an adult in the congregation). Unfortunately, this tutor was of an old school when it came to manner of teaching. Every time Burt made a mistake when reading, he would hit his fingers with a little stick he held in his hand. Well, Burt learned all right, and he performed well at his *bar mitzvah,* in his uncle's temple. But as a result of being mistreated while learning, as soon as the ceremony was over, he never pursued the Hebrew language nor went to temple again, until I came along. Nevertheless, he had a deep religious feeling he carried in his heart at all times both his mother and his father had instilled in him.

## *High School*

While in high school, I found out three important facts so he says in his summary of his life:

> (1) among all the teachers I had, only three knew how to teach and make it interesting, and so were able to impart information; (2) I could beat anyone in a handball game, and I could run a one-hundred-yard dash in almost record time; and (3) there was a shooting range with instructors in firearms, and I became very proficient with a rifle.

> Once while I was doing my running, the running coach approached me to join his track team, telling me he would improve my stride so I could become better than the Olympian Jesse Owens, but I told him that I had to go to my part time jobs because my parents needed the money. At that time, I was very lucky to be employed part-time in a variety of jobs: supermarket bagger and shelf stocker, vegetable and fruit seller, wallpaper hanger, and helper in housing construction. My favorite job was in construction because I made incredible money for a sixteen-year-old boy, part of which I could save for college.

His parents having moved to Wantagh, Long Island from Brooklyn, he lost his three friends, but he made new ones, one in particular, George, who remained his best friend throughout his adulthood. In high school, they would sometimes go to each other's home on a day Burt was not working, and George became fond of Burt's mother and told him often how much he admired her. He was impressed by her always asking them for details of what they had done in school that day and what they had learned while she prepared them snacks to enjoy before they did their homework.


## College

For college, Burt chose Hofstra University because it was somewhat close to where he lived, and at the same time he got accepted there, he landed a job at Abraham & Strauss, a popular and financially sound department store chain. Burt arranged his school hours so he would be able to work a good chunk of time at the store, often having to go to classes in the morning and again in the late afternoons of the same day. This left little time for him to do studying, but he managed to pass all his courses and do well in those he was most interested in like chemistry, physics, and biology. This regimen of work and school was difficult, but he liked his job, made many friends there, and loved some of his courses and, thus, became used to the daily grind. It was that drill that taught him to work hard for the rest of his life.

At A & S, there was a ping-pong table in the basement, and Burt played there sometimes, defeating everyone he played. His superior, seeing this, asked him to play in championship games against the other A & S stores located in the city and nearby. He told me he won every game then too. (This sounded to me as not possible. Years later, I challenged him to a game, not telling him that I was a rather good ping-pong player myself. Well, I got my comeuppance. I never got a single point. The game ended at 21 to 0, and I never played ping-pong against Burt again.)

After graduation, Burt got an offer from Abraham & Strauss, having been liked by all his co-workers and his superiors that was hard to refuse. A partner of the store asked him to stay there full-time, offered him an unbeatable salary, and told him he would be on a line to quickly go up the corporate ladder to eventually become a partner himself. Burt was very tempted, but his love for science won out, so he refused this lucrative offer and went instead for a beginning job in a clinical laboratory. His father was friendly with a dentist whose office was in the same building as the men's clothing store, and he asked him to help Burt get a job. Burt's father was hoping he would study to become a dentist, a profession he saw to be very lucrative, and mentioned this to him occasionally. The dentist was a cousin of the person in charge of the clinical biochemistry laboratory at Memorial Sloan Kettering Cancer Center in New York City, Professor Bodansky, a well-known biochemist who had written the authoritative text on clinical biochemistry. The dentist put in a good word to this cousin, and Burt got a position there.

# 5

## Full-Time Work and Graduate School

And so, it was that Burt was hired at Memorial Sloan Kettering in the clinical chemistry laboratory I had been working at for about two years. I did not pay any attention to him for I was a senior person knowing all there was to know to do there by then and also had established myself as the clown of the place, which gave me major standing, while he had yet to learn the very first tests we ran.

We ran some twenty different biochemical analyses on the blood, spinal fluid, and urine of the patients at the hospital in our clinical laboratory, brought to us by the technicians who drew the blood and collected the other materials. We were also trained to do blood volumes on the patients. For the latter, we had to go up to the patient ourselves, inject a small amount of dye into a vein, then wait for a set time and draw some blood from another vein.

It was the policy of the lab to hire people who were not trained in any of the tests we performed so they would be taught properly by us, and there was no waste of time of unlearning procedures that were different from the way we did them.

At the same time Burt got the job at the laboratory, in Burt's own words,

> I got accepted into a graduate biology pro-
> gram at New York University with a teaching fel-
> lowship. Somehow, I was able to take on both
> positions. The Sloan Kettering position had three
> additional advantages for me: (1) I could earn
> extra money working one night a week and on
> weekends; (2) I became friends with an assistant
> pathologist who would allow me to see autop-
> sies; and (3) on my first day, I saw a pretty and
> funny girl who would become my future wife,
> best friend, and collaborator who, for almost
> sixty years, has allowed us to venture into worlds
> we never dreamed of. After working for a year
> at Memorial, the chief of clinical physiology, Dr.
> Parker Vanamee, asked me if I could work for
> him part-time for extra money and said he would
> clear it with the administration, and I could make
> my own hours. So now I had three paying jobs
> at the same time and a unique girlfriend, who
> was super smart and spoke four languages, which
> became very useful to us later on.

The day Burt was hired, another young man was taken on too, and I did notice that Burt seemed to learn everything much faster than this other new person, and he got his work done in record time. He seemed to catch on very quick to all that had to be done, so in no time at all, he was proficient in all the tests we ran, something I and others took at least a year to learn. He was especially good at doing blood volumes, always finding a vein he could inject and another he could draw from despite these patients having been stuck multiple times during their stay at the hospital, and their veins being in bad shape. He became one of the only two people, out of the eighteen of us, sent to do this test.

As he finished his day's work always in half the time everybody else did, he delighted in sitting on one of our secretaries' desk, talking to her incessantly. One day Willa, one of the secretaries, suggested that he take me out on a date, partly out of kindness to me and partly hoping she would not have to listen to his long discussions anymore.

I was unaware of her promptings and still did not pay much attention to him as he did not look Jewish to me with his straight well-shaped nose (all my relatives had big hook noses) and his Spanish last name. When it was time to share a task with him for a week, as we were wont to do, I was amazed by his strange personality. Besides doing his part of the work very efficiently and incredibly quick, he talked incessantly with me, too, as he had with the secretary. I found that he would pick a topic that piqued his interest and would hold forth without stopping regardless of the fact that I could not con-tribute a word to the conversation. The most amazing thing was that his talk was never boring nor inane. By the end of the week, I had learned more from his *seminars*, as I secretly called them, on many different topics than I had learned in all the years I had been in this country. He spoke about politics, the stock market, DNA, RNA, the *Double Helix* of Watson, who had actually stolen the idea from Rosalind Franklin and Erwin Chargaff, Darwin's discoveries in the Galápagos, and many other "stories" in great detail. By the end of each day, I was surprised not only by how much I had learned from him, but also how little he minded how ignorant I was compared to him, and how I could contribute nothing to the conversation.

At the end of that fateful week, Burt asked me to go out with him to a Chinese restaurant on Long Island, which he knew to serve delicious food, and he promised to order me only the best. I was reluctant as I had my doubts that Chinese food was quite kosher, and furthermore, I did not go out with anyone not Jewish. Well he cleared the latter up, telling me that, yes, he was definitely Jewish—being a descendant of the Jews thrown out of Spain during the Spanish

Inquisition. Burt was the first Sephardic Jew (a Jew whose ancestors came from Spain) I ever met.

Well having that cleared up, I agreed to go with him to the Chinese restaurant in Long Island. We went in his little green car, and that in itself was quite an experience, for the ride was very long according to my standards, and we had to stop every few miles to feed the car's engine oil, or else it would not putter any further. This did not bother Burt one bit, nor did it stop him from holding forth that evening on the topic of his choice, the intricacy of extracting DNA from leukemic cells of mice. He assured me that no one had attempted to do this yet, and that he definitely would be successful at comparing the DNA of those cells with those of normal mice and use that work as a basis for a master's thesis.

When we finally arrived at the restaurant, I dutifully ate Chinese food for the first time, putting out of my mind that it might not have been totally kosher, and found it tasted really good. On the return to New York, we puttered along as before, feeding oil to the little green car's engine and a new topic, the MaCarthy years and the radical left.

After this first date, we fell into a new routine. We started to have lunch together, but went to the cafeteria separately, not to start any gossip among our full of fun and often mischievous sixteen co-workers. Soon, Burt started to come and help me with my work, even if we were not assigned together, because he was always done with his tasks hours before everybody else. Puzzled and incredulous about this unique ability of his, which made me actually suspect he was perhaps faking his results, I observed that he brought an unwavering concentration, an economy of motion, and a clear method of operation to whatever he did, which allowed him to finish his work in half the time it took the ordinary people.

As we both were continuing our education, working toward a master's degree at night, he soon helped me with that too. Calculus, a required course for such a degree, was Greek to me. But pass I did with his patient instructions. On my nights in the lab, a job I had taken on once a week as it was paid handsomely and I enjoyed the challenge, Burt would stay with me, mice and all, working on his master's thesis.

Talking about his work for the master's thesis, Burt said, "Going to graduate school at NYU, I found, luckily, two phenomenal professors namely Paul R. Gross [professor of physiology and molecular biology] and Alexander Sandow [professor of biophysics and director of the New York Muscle Institute]. These individuals delivered the finest, most interesting lectures I have ever been privileged to attend. Both these professors gave such exciting lectures that even if you were sick, you would drag yourself there not to miss them. Eventually, I became so enthralled with biophysics and molecular biology that I became convinced such a combination of disciplines would be extremely useful in understanding and treating various disease states. For my edification, I asked both these teachers would they be mentors for a master's thesis and, hopefully, a PhD in the future. To my amazement, both accepted to sponsor me. Professor Sandow even offered me a job at the Muscle Institute. However, at this early juncture, any commitment on my part would be premature.

Christmas Party picture from our Lab.

At the following Christmas party in our lab, the crew gave me a sizable package as a gift, which I proceeded to unwrap among great laughter by all, finding layers and layers of tissue paper, until at last I came upon a snapshot someone had taken on the sly of me, a five-foot-four-inch person looking up at Burt, a six-foot slender and handsome young man. Our "dating" secret was out.

Life became so different for me. Always reserved in matters of social interactions because of my difficult childhood and past problems, Burt's presence opened up a new world for me. I learned to take pleasure in life: strolling in Central Park, riding in the country, visiting museums, listening to music, always with Burt holding forth with some topic of his choice. He never ran out of topics to talk about, and as time went on, I discovered his secret, he read everything he could get a hold of on subjects that interested him, which were innumerable, and nothing seemed to escape his mind.

I, who had been timid and inexperienced and never really had dated before, slowly became comfortable with him. To my astonishment, without being aware of it, Burt became indispensable to me. I still always wondered what he saw in me to want to continue a relationship with someone so ignorant and burdened with much emotional baggage from the past.

One day, he came down with a bad infection in his mouth that kept him home in Wantagh and prevented him from being able to eat, it was so painful. As I had no car and, anyway, was unable to drive, I had to take a subway, a train, and a bus to reach his home to visit him. Well, he was so grateful that I had taken that long trip and happy to see me. He introduced me to his mom and told her in so many words that I was the girl for him. His mom was not exactly enchanted, but we got along, and I was impressed with her rather aristocratic looks and obvious intelligence. When I left, I promised to come again if he remained sick much longer.

After he came back to work, Burt began asking to tie the knot between us. His patient entreaties were met with steady refusals by me. I wanted to keep him from being burdened with me and the heavy emotional baggage I carried. After four more years of this and him becoming even more insistent, I broke up with him to protect him from myself, being convinced that it was the only kind and fair thing to do. But as a consequence of two unbearably miserable, excruciating days and sleepless nights on my part, I could not rush to work fast enough to admit that if he still would have me, I would marry him; it seemed I could not do without him. And so we became engaged, and six months later, we were married.

# 6

## Marriage and a Master's Degree

We had a small wedding between Christmas and New Year, not to lose time from work and school, in a small temple in the presence of all our colleagues and secretaries, my dad, Burt's parents and two siblings, and a few other relatives of his and mine. Then we went to a honeymoon Burt had arranged in the Poconos, which was delightful as he arranged most everything in our lives from then on. We participated in all the activities offered there: we flew in a helicopter, went for hikes in the mountains, practiced shooting rifles at tin cans, played ping-pong and volleyball with other couples, enjoyed good food seated together with all the other honeymooners, and delighted in the cute cottage—complete with a cozy living room, sporting a lit fire place, a bedroom with an old-fashioned canopy bed, and a Roman bath. Such luxury I had never encountered. Burt was unusually quiet, and I was suffused with a happiness I had never felt before or imagined.

The days went by quickly, but we both enjoyed every minute, a preview of our life together.

Burt moved into the tiny apartment I had previously shared with a roommate from work. It was more like two somewhat large closets and a kitchen and bath, but it was near our work and belonged to Memorial Sloan Kettering, so the rent was minuscule. We were happy, and I felt unbelievably blessed and rich.

The one contribution Burt brought to our place was a record player, we placed on some bricks we had appropriated from the street and oodles of records of classical music he loved. His knowledge of music was such that he had the ability to name a piece that was being played on the radio or anywhere from just the first few notes he heard. He often even knew who was conducting, and, of course, who the soloist was that was playing.

After having taken the necessary courses for the master's thesis, it was time for Burt to do the research and, first (in his own words), to find a suitable sponsor who would accept me and offer me research work I was most interested in. Asking Professor Gross whether he would sponsor me still, as he had alluded to when I first started the program, he gladly agreed.

Having access to free animals, their care and boarding as well as strains of leukemic mice, I decided to investigate possible nucleotide base and structural changes in DNA from leukemic cells of mice versus those of normal mice. Since I was working at three different jobs, I had to do all the experiments from about 10 p.m. to the early morning hours and on weekends. Because some of the assays for this study were not available, I had to first develop a few new biochemical and biophysical assays, which turned out to be quite interesting, exciting, and a lot of fun. My eventual results did, indeed, show changes in some of the nucleotide bases and structures. So the difficult lab work was clearly worth the effort. It then came time to write up the thesis. This, too, was fun for me. Although, after a lot of effort, I felt my write-up was a fairly good one, Professor Gross desired me to make many changes, which, of course, I did. However, after two more rewrites, Professor Gross indicated a need for more changes. So I said, "Why don't you write it yourself now!". He answered me I was quite an upstart since none of his previous students ever said such a thing to him. However, he then surprised me and said, "I think it is okay now." So I won that little skirmish and was awarded my M.Sc. degree.

# 7

## On to a PhD

Professor Gross was offered a great position at Brown University in Rhode Island at that time and asked Burt to move there, too, to continue his studies for a PhD. Burt told him it was a great offer, but since he had a new bride who was studying in New York for her PhD, it would be difficult to move to Rhode Island. Surprisingly, Professor Gross offered to get her into a doctoral program of her choosing at Brown. This was a fantastic effort on his part, but we decided to stay in New York.

This now posed a dilemma. Where and to whom would I go for a new sponsor in molecular biology/biophysics? Professor Gross suggested I speak with Professor Teru Hayashi, one of the "shining lights" in molecular biology/biophysics at Columbia University. At first glance, this seemed to be a great move for me. However, when I was interviewed by Professor Hayashi, I found he misquoted numerous research papers, reports, and data analyses during our conversation. He became extremely annoyed when I tried to correct his "mistakes" and quoted journal titles, authors, exact years of publication, and inclusive pages to him. Telling him to check my corrections and references pleased him even less. Our bantering went on until I got up, thanked him for the interview, and left. So my possibility to go to Columbia went "down the tubes." The next day, I got a phone call from Professor Gross in which he said that Hayashi did check my quoted references and that I was correct on all counts. Hayashi also told him that he thought, at first, I was insulting him, but I stood my ground, which he admired. He proceeded to say that he wanted me as a student and offered me a fine fellowship if I would join him. He did say he could not understand how I could recite all the references so accurately. [Only my wife knew that I had a photographic memory. She was in awe of this ability God had given me.] I mulled over Hayashi's kind offer but rejected it. It did not look like a fruitful working combination to me.

Where to go next? I decided to proceed to the Department of Pathology at New York University School of Medicine. After interviewing with as many scientists as would give me the opportunity, I decided to accept an offer from Professor Benjamin Zweifach, the dean of microcirculation [comprised of blood vessels that are too small to be seen without a microscope]. His publications on inflammation, shock and trauma, and circulatory control mechanisms sparked my interest and excitement, so I accepted his offer coming with a nice fellowship.

Learning to see the microcirculation

I proceeded to learn and master new techniques in studying the microcirculation, circulatory control mechanisms, and mechanisms involved in development and treatment of inflammation, shock and trauma.

Burt, thus, continued his studies beyond his master's degree full-time in the pathology department of New York University, having gotten a fellowship, and as for me, I remained working in the lab, also taking courses at night toward a PhD.

Professor Zweifach and I decided to study the roles of histamine in microcirculatory control of peripheral blood flow, inflammation, and circulatory shock. We rattled a few movers in this field with our results. Needless to say, I received my PhD in record time, which resulted in six major articles in good scientific and medical journals. [Most PhD students are lucky to get one full-length paper from their thesis, and most PhD students take from four to six years to complete their degree.] During the three years I was working in Professor Zweifach's lab, unbeknownst to me, several scientists were asking about me and my studies. Three of these people, including Professor Furchtgott [a future Nobelist], offered me either a postdoctoral fellowship or an opportunity to run a lab in the investigation of mechanisms and treatment of circulatory shock and trauma. One of the latter offered, in addition, a large research grant, several research associates, technicians, and a bona fide faculty position at three times the salary of the postdoctoral offers. I could not resist this chance. It afforded me the title of an associate director of research in the Department of Anesthesiology at New York University School of Medicine under the directorship of Professor Solomon Hershey, an anesthesiologist and shock and trauma specialist. In addition, it entailed also getting a laboratory and appointment in the offices of the New York City Medical Examiner, all these riches, and me right out of graduate school. This position at NYU School of Medicine and at the medical examiner's labs were the beginning of my career. It not only afforded me the studies I did under the direction and collaboration of Professor Hershey, who had a very fertile mind brimming with ideas, but also the opportunity to investigate some of my own hypotheses.

# 8

## The Beginning of a Career

Professor Hershey and I were interested in exploring whether (1) some drugs could act differently depending on which part of the microcirculation was tested namely arterioles, precapillary sphincters, metarterioles, or venules; (2) was it possible to stimulate the immune system to where it could be useful in the treatment and prevention of diverse forms of circulatory shock and trauma; and (3) could phagocytic indices of macrophages [the ability of certain white cells to engulf bacteria, viruses, and other foreign material] be used to assess tissue functions in shock and trauma.

We turned out to be right on all our speculations we studied.

(1) With the aid of several peptide chemists at Sandoz Pharmaceuticals, the Czech Academy of Sciences, and Mount Sinai Medical School, we directed the synthesis of alterations in the molecular structures of vasopressin and oxytocin [two hormones, which among other things also affect the circulation] based on their constrictor/dilator actions on different microvessels, which gave us

interesting results particularly in venules.[3,4,5] Our findings resulted in benefits in the treatment of different forms of experimental shock and trauma.

(2) Using diverse forms of molecules and drugs, we were able to stimulate the innate immune system, which resulted in increased survival rates of animals subjected to shock and trauma.[6,7,8] These studies led me to the discovery of what I believe is the body's major host defense factor, which I termed HDFx.

After a few years as the work progressed, which resulted in my writing many scientific papers in prestigious journals, I began to get offers from all over the country to become a chairman of a physiology department or even biochemistry and physiology department or director of a group of scientists interested in what I was doing in faraway places like Genentech in California, the University of Michigan, the University of Chicago in Illinois, Rutgers University in New Jersey, Cornell University in Upstate New York, the University of North Carolina, and Emory in Georgia. I went for interviews to most places but even got an appointment in one place, sight unseen, right over the telephone. It was an amazing development, and I was torn between accepting some of these offers, as the prestige and the money involved where out of sight. Well, my wife wanted us to stay in New York City because we had a daughter by then, who was going to elementary school, and due to her remembering how hard it was for her to change school so often as she had to do, she wanted to spare our daughter that difficulty. It was a very hard decision, but in New York we stayed. [What an incredible sacrifice I, later, could not forgive myself for.]

# 9

## Professor of Physiology, Pharmacology, and Medicine

I accepted a position at the State University of New York, Downstate Medical Center in Brooklyn, New York, with more lab space, a somewhat better salary and a tenured full professor title at the age of thirty-five.

During the negotiations with the chairman of the Physiology department, Dr. Vahe Amassian, he offered my wife a position that would lead to tenure, too, if she would teach medical students for a period of several months each year. But since she had never taught before, she was reluctant to accept it, so her salary would have to come from my grants. Since I had several grants at the time, this was not a problem [sacrifice number 2].

One of my grants was given me for the purpose of studying the effect of alcohol, illicit and psychedelic drugs on vascular smooth muscle [muscle from blood vessels] and the micro-circulation of the brain. Every mind-altering drug tested [i.e., LSD, PCP, psilocybin, heroin, among others] caused contraction of cerebral vascular muscle, leading us to believe this was the prime reason these drugs produce hallucinations and strokes.[9,10] Later on, using in vivo microcirculatory observations on cerebral and medullary microvessels, we confirmed that these mind-altering drugs could induce vasoconstriction with rupture of post-capillary venules and bleeding into the brain tissue. We found that alcohol could induce similar cerebral vascular actions and strokes if given in large enough concentrations.[11] In all these cases, using P-NMR spectroscopy, [nuclear magnetic resonance, a method to identify organic compounds], we found that the psychedelics and alcohol would cause fall in intracellular free magnesium, ATP [adenosine triphosphate], ADP [adenosine diphosphate], and a rise in inorganic phosphate just prior to their stroke-like effect, a clear sign of destruction of cells.

# 10

## A New Project

It just so happened that Burt came into a discovery by sheer serendipity, as sometimes happens. Studying pieces of aortic smooth muscle, which was done always in a so-called normal Ringer's solution that is a solution that contains all the minerals found in blood in the same amounts as they are found in healthy individuals and kept at body temperature. Ringer had found that tissues studied in this solution could be kept for hours and experimented on without any deterioration of the tissue or other problems.

One day, Burt making up such a solution had left out one of the minerals by mistake, and as he studied the tissue, he found that the piece of rat aorta gave him strange results—that is (1) the tissue would contract all by itself instead of sitting peacefully stretched out in the bath; (2) when he added contractile drugs, the tissue reacted more forcefully than usual; but (3) when he added relaxant drugs, the tissue would not relax.

Since when making any solution, it is customary to write down in a special book what we add and in what amount, he soon found his mistake and was amazed at the results. Curiosity does not kill the cat in research. Curiosity is the mover and sine qua non of research. Burt knew that magnesium, the mineral he had omitted in making the Ringer's solution, had many effects on over three hundred enzymes, but no one had studied this mineral's effect in the circulation or in the heart for that matter. And so, he asked me to repeat his preliminary serendipitous "study" knowing full well that I would do it a thousand times over before reporting on it. As it happened, his chance discovery turned out to be one of our major contributions. We studied the effects of Mg deficiency and normal presence on different blood vessels and the heart and found that it was a very important mineral for health. Although epidemiological studies in the past (findings in people living in areas known to be deficient in magnesium in food and water) had pointed to this fact, no one had ever made a study of its effect on the cardiovascular system. We proceeded to do that; it turned out to give us a wealth of information and kept us happy for years. A medical technology company in Massachusetts, Nova Biomedical, prepared a special electrode for us with which we could study the entity of magnesium that affect tissues directly, namely the ionized part, and so we were able to measure the amount of magnesium in the blood of healthy and diseased people accurately. We found that ionized magnesium was reduced in the blood of patients right after a heart attack, in about fifty percent of patients with stress headaches or migraines and in pregnant women who suddenly developed an increased blood pressure. We found that all these patients could benefit by either an infusion of magnesium sulfate directly and/or by oral supplementation of this mineral.

A most interesting study we did was with patients getting liver or kidney transplants. Some of these patients suffered from sudden heart attacks, although their transplants remained in good conditions. We were the first to show that these patients exhibited some of the lowest amounts of ionized magnesium in their blood because of their having to take cyclosporin daily to prevent organ rejection.

Finally, we engaged in a study with rats whom we gave food containing only ten percent of magnesium of their normal food but added different amounts of the mineral in their drinking water, carefully measuring the amounts they drank each day. This showed us the minimum amount of the mineral necessary for health, at least in rats. We have been most gratified that this study led to a large long-term study instituted by Prime Minister Benjamin Netanyahu and his health minister in Israel in May of 2012 in a region that uses only desalinated drinking water. They added magnesium to their drinking water according to our specification and are following the inhabitants' health in terms of various criteria like blood pressure, heart attacks, strokes, etc.

# 11

# HDFx

Ever since Burt's early work with Professor Hershey on shock and trauma, where they explored stimulation of the immune system with various drugs, he was interested in pursuing this possibility by other means and remained intrigued with that idea. He had wanted to explore why some people were resistant to stress and survived different diseases while others did badly or did not survive. He saw endless possibilities affecting health if the native immune system could indeed be stimulated enough to ameliorate the outcome. He carefully reread Dr. Hans Selye's work who was the founder of the stress theory. He was the first to recognize the communality of responses to noxious stimuli in what he called the general adaptation syndrome.[12] Burt then reread the work by Metchnikoff E. who discovered phagocytosis (the engulfing of bacteria, viruses, and other material by three different white blood cells) and is considered the father of cell-mediated immunity.[13]

With Burt's first, rather crude, experiments stressing mice by simple means and collecting their blood, he discovered that those animals who were unaffected by the stress and surviving it had something in their blood, which could be transferred to other mice to make them tolerate the same stress. After many repetitions of these experiments, which gave identical results, he tried other stressors and found similar effects. Animals who were stressed by various means, like blood loss or body trauma, and survived the stress produced something in their blood that could make other animals resist the stress and, lo and behold, different stressors as well. Burt found that he could increase the immune system so much that animals would be resistant to diseases they usually succumbed to. It was a revelation well worth pursuing. After many more such experiments, it was time to find the actual agent or agents, which allowed such results. Burt got as far as realizing that the material was a protein, but he did not have the money it would take to study its makeup. The cost of such a study would be prohibitive for a simple grant.

After much cogitation and agonizing, Burt spoke to two friends who knew how to raise money in the corporate world. They counseled him to raise the money by going to various foundations and tell them about this infinitely worthy, exciting, and invaluable health-promoting subject.

He consulted with a congressional representative from Brooklyn, the honorable Charles Rangel, who advised him to try some of the foundations he knew about, so he presented his work to several political groups like the Clinton Foundation, who turned him down. He talked to the NIH (National Institute of Health), Dr. Fauci's domain, who also turned him down. Burt did not have the kind of, shall we say to be kind, *savoir faire* (i.e., diplomacy or standing in the world) that would appeal to such people (see chapter 12).

He consulted with two members of the SUNY Research Foundation, Admiral John Craine, and Nicholas Rostow, who referred him to the Naval Research Center where he met with Drs. Ed Antosek, Al Mateczun, and Kurt Henry. He visited the National Science Council, where he met with Mr. Juan Zarate. He consulted with the National Institute of Allergy and Infectious Diseases, where he spoke with Dr. Michael Kurilla. He approached the Defense Research Projects Agency (DARPA), where he interacted with Dr. Brett Giroir.

Most of everyone he spoke to became excited. Burt's enthusiasm was infectious to all those he gave presentations to. They were all willing to help and give him the money, but there was always a problem of Burt's own doing: he did not want to share any part of his research accomplishment with anyone.

Burt moved heaven and earth to try to find a group of people who would not ask for and demand sharing the work. He did not want to give up any part of his arduous, demanding, and time-consuming research to anyone or share it in any way. He wanted to be sole owner and administrator of his "baby," but this was not a realistic way of doing business.

Burt went to the British Embassy in Washington, where he met with a kind gentleman, Dr. Andy Trethewey. He got introduced to a Lord Hanson, who was totally taken by Burt and the research and arranged a trip for us to Porton Down near Salisbury, England, a government military set of laboratories.

Since he was going to be using bacteria and/or viruses, he went to places that were equipped to handle those safely. Therefore, he went to labs which had BSL-4 levels of security (a lab where potentially deadly infectious agents were handled). This included DARPA of the US Department of Defense and Porton Down in England.

Most of the places he went to were ready to give him the money and help if he would let them be equal partners with him, but Burt could not agree to such an arrangement. In accordance with his nature (see chapter 12), he secretly wanted to eventually give the material free to anyone who needed it, which he figured no one spending the kind of money it would require could possibly agree to.

He finally found two individuals who were going to let him do it his way, not demanding any stake in the research: the head of a pharmaceutical firm in Switzerland who was willing to go along with him and promised him enough money to get him started, and Lord Hanson from England, who had the wealth to give freely. It was not meant to be. Both of these gentlemen passed away shortly thereafter, before the arrangements were consummated. But Burt never gave up. He still hoped to eventually get this so important research accomplished.

It is well-known that a vaccine, like the vaccines against coronavirus, is specific only for that particular virus. As a result, when there is a change in virus occurring like a mutation, the immune system will work only against the original virus and would be impotent against any new virus.

HDFx would, therefore, definitely be a much better agent than a vaccine.

# 12

## A Man Like No Other

Burt had a heart of gold. As soon as we were reasonably comfortable financially, he donated money to all causes he felt needed it. He gave money regularly to children's hospitals like the Shriners Hospital for Children, the St. Jude Children's Research Hospital; he donated to Wounded Warriors Project, Veterans of Foreign Wars; and he researched American Indian tribes to donate to those who were poor and suffered from diseases and to their schools for scholarships. He donated to the Dakota Indian Foundation, the American Indian College Fund, the Southwest Reservation Aid, the St. Joseph's Indian School. He did this continually, and so he was showered with little presents. We had a colorful Lakota dream catcher on every door of our house and then some. He also got invitations to go to graduations and special events. He donated to many other causes, orphanages, boys and girls' clubs, children who were born with cleft palates, several charities to Israel, and when needs came up because of special circumstances like earthquakes and hurricanes.

He also supported generously people running for office he liked and was sure would keep this country on the right path. Lately, he donated to President Trump, our two senators and our governor and local representatives he approved of.

He kept himself and me informed by getting up with the birds and reading late at night the newspapers he bought daily, the magazines and journals he had sent to the house by mail, and Internet sites he followed religiously. He read the *Wall Street Journal*, the *New York Post*, the *Washington Times*, the *Financial Times* of London, the local papers, *Breitbart News*, the *Drudge Report*, and the *Limbaugh Letter*. He read at least twice as fast as I could, so he kept me informed about all important matters, as the first thing out of my mouth every morning was "what's new?"

A very unique and strangely beneficial characteristic of his was that when he got angry at something, which was not very often, instead of stewing over it or letting it interfere with his work, on the contrary, he would work harder, longer, and in a more concentrated manner. In other words, when angry, he got over it by working more. I admired that quality in him to no end and could not understand how he had developed it into an art.

As to his family, after having spent time and effort with care and love, when the brothers were small, especially the younger one who was ten years his junior, he now would talk to either one of them, at great length, having not seen them in months. Whenever they called him, usually for a health-related problem, he would counsel them, and inevitably soon after, a lively conversation would ensue about the New York Mets baseball team and their latest exploits. They all remained faithful to that team no matter how they were doing and no matter which state the brothers lived in now.

Burt with his daughter at her graduation from Medical School.

And our daughter, whom he adored from the moment she was born and spent an inordinate amount of time, care, and money for[2], he gladly let her call him in the middle of the night to help her solve one of her financial or work-related problems. This he did even if she had not talked to him for ages, not even for his last birthday being super busy, which he was sad about (shades of his relation with his father, only in reverse).

He always had time for our twenty-one-year-old granddaughter, Rebecca[2], whom he still called sweetie pie, to discuss at great length her future in science and college plans and never forgot to mention how much he loved her wonderful ability to paint, and how grateful he was for that one last painting she made for him he kept in his line of view.

Of course, he would talk to David[2], our eighteen-year-old grandson, a budding musician, of the classical music they both loved, and David never ceased to be amazed at his grandpa's knowledge, all the composers and pieces of music he knew about, and his understanding of similarities of some composer's music to another's. He made him promise to go to the better of two colleges David was considering, and so he did follow his wish.

As for our son-in-law, he dubbed him an angel for the selfless way he was and still is always there for us.

An unintended unhelpful quality Burt had was at meetings here in the US when he got up to make a comment, saying something like "on page 665 of Circulation Research 1973, volume 32, Dr. B. disagrees with your conclusions. Could you be mistaken?" This kind of thing made him appear very arrogant. People usually could quote papers by author and journal. No one remembered volume numbers, dates, and certainly not pages.

Burt had one fault, which was detrimental to him he was totally unaware of. He did not know how to be diplomatic and certainly not for his own benefit. He said whatever had to be said without embellishment. He did not know how to make small talk and especially how to endear himself to anybody to get something in return; that was a total no-no to him. He never made friends with the higher-ups of the university, never mixed with the deans or the president and vice president of the school.

And so it was that we lost a chance to work on a big project with China. We had been the first lab in our university to have several Chinese scientists come and work with us in the US. Four senior scientists came to stay with us for several years and then returned to their schools. One postdoc came and remained with us, intent to stay in the US. We became good friends with all these people. They were hardworking and grateful to us, and we usually made parties in our home, which they were not used to, they were rather private people, but got to enjoy our ways.

A party at our home.

# 13

# China

One of the scientists who was a dean in his university invited us to come to China for an extensive trip in which Burt gave talks in several of their universities faraway from each other. It was a pleasure to watch him talk. He would say several sentences, wait for them to be translated, and then continue, never losing his place, never becoming flustered or confused. He did that even if he was jet-lagged from the long trips or tired from having prepared the talk for the next day, staying up most of the night. I was so proud of him.

After this extensive trip and their very gracious hosting, the higher-ups of one of the Beijing universities decided to cooperate with our school and have Burt be the liaison in an extended exchange program of scientists and postdocs and, in addition, send over different herbs they had studied and found to be effective against different diseases. Our university would be engaged in analyzing these herbs to find the active ingredients. We were honored and excited about this plan. When it came time for the elite of the Beijing University to visit our school, the president of our university refused to greet them or even see them. He sent an underling to say that we were not going to be in a position to accommodate them or work with them. We were dumbfounded. Since Burt was never part of the inner circle, we never found out the official reason for this outcome. But I knew full well that Burt, who had never broken bread with the higher-ups and never schmoozed with them or took them out to dinner or in any way ingratiated himself to them, simply was not the kind of person these people were going to give such a high honor to. The university lost a great financial boon since the collaboration was all going to be paid for by China.

Lo and behold, the monies and studies wound up in the National Institutes of Health with Professor Dr. Fauci, the beneficiary.

# 14

## The Life of a Scientist

Apart of being a scientist is to go to scientific meetings, and the more you become known, the more meetings you get invited to. These meetings give you a chance to present your work to as many other scientists as you can, not only to show what has been done in the field but also to get input from others on how to continue and to hear what new studies have been done by them in your field of interest. It is a cross-fertilization of ideas and hypotheses that help formulate new thoughts and new work.

We worked hard at these meetings. In the morning and afternoon, we sat and listened to several scientists each present their latest work for a set amount of time, always leaving time for questions. The meetings usually lasted for a minimum of three to five days, four hours in the morning and four to five hours in the afternoon, and one had to concentrate to grasp new concepts and often new twists and turns of previous facts.

Burt always was in his element at these meetings. During the time between the official meetings, he made many good friends, especially abroad, and it gave him a chance to talk to his heart's content, usually surrounded with a group of interested parties. Some of these friends came to our lab for a period of time and others collaborated with us long distance.

In front of a mural with a friend in Japan

We went to Paris and Lisbon, Brussels and Budapest, Stockholm and Copenhagen, Rome and Florence, London and Athens, Crete and Jerusalem, Hawaii, and different cities in Japan and China. We never had to pay our way anywhere, the hosts covered our expenses. We were treated as royalty partly because of our work we presented and partly because we were Americans. Burt always gave at least one talk in each place we went to, sometimes more, and I often gave one too. Burt was able to give hour-long talks, just having little crib notes in his hand with single words of topics to be discussed, while I had to have my whole talk written out in detail. Not to get me distracted, lose my place in the talk, and get confused, Burt would point to the projected material I was discussing.

Giving a talk in Paris while Burt points to the projected picture.

There were other places we went to, like Leuven in Belgium, Zurich and Geneva in Switzerland, and castles in the Loire Valley in France. Each place had wonderful charm, and the hosts did their best to make us comfortable and happy.

Burt organized several meetings in California, one each in Los Angeles, San Diego, and Ventura.

Giving lectures in Japan, China, France and Hungary

In Burt's words,

Our many published findings have led us to deliver invited lectures in many countries [as seen above] and gave us a slew of postdoctoral fellows to join our research team, and we obtained numerous research grants from NHLBI, NIMH, NIAAA, and NIDA as well as pharmaceutical companies. However, along the way, it is important to impart that there were many frustrations and setbacks in writing research grants, waiting to hear back comments from reviewers and finding out that our funding requests were reduced or often even not awarded. I have been blessed by the Lord by having a brilliant wife, best friend, and great collaborator who has often not been given the credit she deserves. All of our postdoctoral fellows looked upon Bella as a surrogate mother, helper with their problems, and good friend who they often would seek out because she would never turn them down when her help was needed. Although I am the author of almost 1,100 complete, full-length, peer-reviewed articles, reviews, and editorials, I could not have accomplished our studies without my ever hardworking wife, the research associates, postdocs, and fantastic technicians who deserve much of the credit for our accomplishments.

Our lab: Dr. K. Huang from China, A. Gebrewold from Ethiopia, Dr. T. Murakawa from Japan, A. Carella from Italy, Burt and me.

Sometimes as a consequence of one's research, you are lucky enough to be honored by being elected a fellow of prestigious societies. In my case, I have been elected as a fellow by the Royal Society of Medicine, the American Association for the Advancement of Science, the American Heart Association, the American Board of Forensic Medicine, the Association of Clinical Scientists, the American Institute of Chemists, and the Cardiovascular Section of the American Physiological Society. In addition, I was named as "State University Inventor of the Year".

An unexpected reward was that my wife and I were honored with a gold medal by the French Academy of Medicine for our work in nutrition and a bronze medal by the former president of France, Jacques Chirac, for furthering Franco-American scientific relations. We obtained the Mildred Seelig Award for Outstanding Contributions to Research on the Role of Magnesium in Health and Disease. Lastly, we obtained a first Israeli Hippocrates Award complete with a beautiful silver statuette for our contributions to that country.

Due to being author and co-author of almost 1,100 complete, full-length, peer-reviewed articles, reviews, and editorials, I am on the editorial board of more than fifty journals in cardiology, medicine, biochemistry, physiology, pharmacology, toxicology, histology, pulmonology, anesthesiology, cell biology, molecular biology, and immunology.

I have also served at the NIH, American Heart Association, and NSF [National Science

Foundation] study sections to review other scientists' grants.

Burt ended the summary of his life at the age of eighty thusly:

> From my life's experiences, I have learned several important things to be handed down to those who are young and about to enter a career: (1) do not expect any goals to be achieved without hard work and toil; (2) if you believe in something strongly, do not give in until proven wrong no matter what the opposition declares; (3) be willing to learn new things even if, at first, the task looks unachievable; (4) always pursue your dreams no matter how difficult the path seems; and (5) be lucky enough to find a loving mate.

# 15

## Life without My Husband

I have been inconsolable, full of grief. I blame myself for many things I had not done for Burt. I blame myself for having insisted to leave the country and asking Burt to renew my passport. I especially blame myself for that moment I went to brush my teeth instead of making breakfast for him first. I blame myself for not having encouraged him to go to one of the universities or places, which had offered him chairmanships and great remunerations. I blame myself for not having made the effort to teach to obtain a tenured track when we first went to SUNY Downstate. I blame myself for many other things and not having told him enough times how much I loved him.

Unable to walk and believing I would remain crippled for all time, being totally dependent on the kindness and hard work of my son-in-law Michael, I decided, on the spur of the moment and full of grief and misery, to sell my home and move into a senior facility near the cemetery where Burt was to be able to be near him.

Without a reasonable, sensible working brain, I entered into the venture of selling our beautiful home we both had loved, signing on to a single real estate agent. As should have been expected, I got what I deserved. Deciding a major undertaking at a time I was in no condition to think clearly, see clearly, and respond clearly, I got cheated right and left. I got cheated out of most of our possessions, being an old woman half out of her mind with grief. Burt's thousands of books, some with great value, and his beautiful music in the form of innumerable records and CDs were taken over by a man hired by the real estate people who made me pay a fortune under the name of "getting rid of junk." All these precious and beloved treasures were simply thrown out of the window into a large trash bin. I paid another fortune for putting mulch in our surrounding landscape and for pulling a few plants out that had been damaged by Hurricane Irma several years past and had not recovered. The real estate agent insisted on hiring a man for that job too. That same man had been doing our landscape for many years, never once repairing nor replacing the plants we paid him to take care of. I was also asked to pay $10,500 to a potential buyer for repairs, for our house, which was in mint condition, other than some minor problems I had estimated to be fixed with a cost of $200. I was made to leave the home I loved in a great hurry in order to empty the house so it could be shown to potential buyers. At first, they said I had to leave in three days, but when I finally let myself be heard by screaming hysterically that I could not possibly do that, they "allowed" me two more days. Still, I forgot to take with me so many valuable things, even things I would need every day. A kind friend helped me without whom I would not have made it at all, but I forgot much still. This stress all added to my inability to function, so much so, that I relied on my son-in-law who is a kind soul and was rather accommodating to the real estate people, not to get into any kind of altercation with them.

I could not cope at all. Burt had done everything for me during the sixty years we were married. I did not know how to pay bills and what my financial situation was. I could not concentrate and left it all for Michael to do.

# 16

## Mr. Biden

At first, I did not listen to the news, but soon I could not help myself being witness to the utter destruction of my golden America.

On January 20, 2021, on the very first day the guy was in office, thousands of jobs were taken from American citizens by executive order, stopping the construction of the Keystone XL Pipeline that was bringing in oil from Canada to the US at a cheap rate. This pipeline had been kicked around for years by Obama[1]. By executive order, one by one, he stopped and reversed all the good things President Trump had instituted, reinstituting all the regulations that would stimy small businesses, joining the Paris Accords to ameliorate the "worst problem America was facing"—global warming. He rejoined the Iran deal and got rid of the sanctions against Iran so they could continue shamelessly their quest for atomic bombs. Worse yet, he stopped building the wall in the southern border of our country and reversed the deal President Trump had made with Mexico, so he let in millions of illegals, riddled with COVID-19 and many other diseases; invited in illegal drugs, criminal elements, sex trafficking. He approved the taking away of substantial money from the police and diminished the military. This all was done in a matter of days, the fastest destruction possible of our beloved country.

Crime, killings, and open lootings of fine stores were the order of the day in democratically led cities and suburbs. The homeless, drug-addicted population grew there by leaps and bounds, and the counts of the people shot each day was a new statistical exercise. Chicago came in first, followed by New York City, and cities in Minnesota. Biden and his crew outdid themselves daily with things that were destructive to our country. There was no end to the iniquities that were going on. Trillions of dollars were to be given out for purposes that had nothing to do with the things they were meant for like the repair of roads, bridges, and airports that were falling apart and for compensation to people whose livelihood was badly affected by COVID. Instead, most of the money would be going to pet projects of the democratic leaders like Nancy Pelosi—just like Obama had done when he first came into office. He had allocated tons of taxpayer money for what he called the stimulus bill[1], a bill that was thousands of pages long as was the one crafted by the democrats now. Around that time came the famous dictum from Mrs. Pelosi: "You have to pass the bill before you read it," a piece of wisdom that has to go down in history. Criminals were let out of jail, they were debating increasing the number of supreme court justices, doing away with the filibuster, never instituting term limits, and for heaven's sake, never touching the way of electing people that had worked so well for Biden. Getting picture IDs and not having elections by mail for weeks would be the worst racism possible.

Talking about *racism* that word was bandied about shamelessly, and this country was being pushed back by a hundred years. Everything the democrats did not like was due to racism. Worst of all, they instituted teaching little children to become racists by telling them that whites were oppressors and blacks were victims. Statues were being taken down that were part of history because they were deemed racist.

Another thing the democrats pursued with zest was sex. Little five-year-old children were going to be taught in school about homosexuality and gender changes. It was truly the devil himself leading America. Neighbors were being taught to spy on neighbors, and family units were deemed unnecessary. In fact, teens were taught to stand up to their parents and demand their due, or else they could take them to court and sue them for it.

The language was being destroyed because of the insistence of transgender craze. The words *mother* and *father* were banned. Instead, they were called birthing people. Much of what went on I had to tune myself out of. It was too much to bear.

And Biden had a ball with the COVID-19. It was "wear masks and be vaccinated," "be vaccinated and wear masks," and "wear masks and be vaccinated," ad nauseum. He finally declared a mandate for people to be vaccinated who worked in places that included more than one hundred people companies, but the post office workers and congress people and their staff were exempted from this command. This mandate included the teachers, the military, the police, the first responders, and the nurses and doctors in hospitals. If you were not vaccinated, you were simply going to lose your job. The national guard was elected to fill in.

Until a little hitch came into the mix of continuing the destruction of America, and Biden made it worldwide. He decided to take the troops out of Afghanistan. He announced the date loud and clear, by August 31 the military would be out of that country. Well, he did not count on the Taliban, Al Qaida, and ISIS. Biden got the military out first. He left eighty-four million dollars' worth of weapons, rifles, guns, large equipment, trucks, helicopters, body armor and uniforms, and the latest of planes as presents for the terrorists. There had been no plan to do it right, to make sure American civilians and the friendly Afghans, who had helped us in that twenty-year war, would come to safety first. A suicide bomber decided to do his thing near the airport of Kabul, the capital of Afghanistan, and thirteen of our finest young marines and navy people died, many others were injured, and hundreds of Afghans died and got injured. It was a sad and shameful day for the administration, but they tried to spin it as the perils of war and ultimately, of course, it was President Trump's fault.

Biden needed to do something drastic after the suicide bombing to show who was in charge. So he announced with his secretary of defense that they had been successful in destroying a big leader of one of the terrorist groups. As soon as this was said, I knew it must be a lie. Sure enough, a week or so after bragging of this deed, it came out that we had killed seven children and three adult civilians in that attack, a colossal horror and shame.

On August 31, the evacuation stopped, leaving Americans behind who could not make it to the planes and leaving many Afghans friendly to us behind at the mercy of the Taliban and all the other terrorists armed to the teeth with the latest equipment thanks to Biden and whoever was guiding him on. Not only that, but the terrorists were in possession of a list of names given to them by us, of Americans, and Afghans who had helped us and were left behind. The Taliban were celebrating their mighty victory while we were retreating in shame.

Women were immediately treated as they had been before under Sharia law, they could not get jobs, could not go out alone, girls could not go to school, and we saw them being beaten, mistreated, and even killed on some videos smuggled out of that country.

Biden declared with pride on TV that the retreat out of Afghanistan was a huge success.

The latest news is that while our border in the south is left wide open, letting in criminals, diseases, drugs, trafficking of women and minors, Mr. Biden is intent on helping Ukraine and Taiwan keep their borders secure and intact. He is sending our boys and girls in the military to eastern Europe to help Ukraine. It is a disaster waiting to happen. Some say it may turn into WWIII.

As of this writing, Ukraine turned into a killing field with women and children, the preferred victims. The dead were buried in mass graves. Many Ukrainians, who were able to, became refugees running to various European countries, especially Poland. In addition, the Iran nuclear deal was pursued by the administration to its fullest, putting both Israel and the US in dire danger to be wiped out.[14,15]

# Epilogue

My hip has healed, and I am able to walk again thanks to some professional physical therapists. So I go to the cemetery once a week—the only place I do not feel utterly and inexorably alone, and I speak to Burt. I tell him how much I miss him, I tell him how much I love him, and I beg his forgiveness, again and again, for all the things I did not do for him and all the things I did wrong.

# Acknowledgments

I would like to thank Michael Holloway, our son-in-law, for all the kind and supportive things he did for Burt and myself in our many days of need.

I would like to thank my friend Judy Chezar from Israel, who has repeatedly urged me to write this book and has thus given me a reason to live, albeit temporarily.

# Notes

1. Altura, B. T., *What Difference Does It Make? What Happened to Our Country* (Create Space, 2017).
2. Altura, B. T., *Golden America*, (New York: Page, 2014).
3. Trump, D. J., *Our Journey Together.* (Winning Team Publishing, 2021).
4. Altura, B. M., and S. G. Hershey, *Bulletin of the New York Academy of Medicine* 43 (1967): 259–266.
5. Altura, B. M., *Journal of Pharmacology and Experimental Therapeutics* (1976): 187–196.
6. Altura, B. M., and Altura, B. T., *Federation Proceedings* 36, no. 6 (1977): 1853–1860.
7. Altura, B. M., and Altura, B. T., *Journal of Pharmacology and Experimental Therapeutics* 193, no. 2 (1975): 413–423.
8. Altura, B. M., and B. T. Altura, *Alcoholism: Clinical and Experimental Research* 18, no. 5 (1994): 1057–1068.
9. Altura, B. M., B. T. Altura, and A. Gebrewold, *Science* 230 (1983): 331–333.
10. Altura, B. T., R. Quirion, B. Pert, and B. M. Altura, *Proceedings of the National Academy of Sciences of the United States of America* 80, no. 3 (1983): 865–869.
11. Selye, H., "A Syndrome Produced by Diverse Noxious Agents," *Nature* 138 (1936): 32.
12. Metchnikoff E. *Immunity in Infectious Diseases.* (Cambridge University Press, Boston, 1905).
13. *Washington Examiner*, a weekly magazine.

14. Schweizer, P. *Red-Handed*. Harper Collins, New York. (2022).
15. Hannity, Sean. The Hannity program on Fox News TV, 9:00 p.m. every weekday.

# About the Author

The author was born in Germany at the beginning of the Nazi era. She and her parents managed to escape concentration camp shortly after experiencing Kristallnacht and wandered through Belgium, France, and Switzerland for ten years, succeeding to escape the Germans. They finally were allowed to come to "golden America" after peace was established thanks to the US military and the efforts of Russia.

Losing her mother to cancer shortly after entering the promised land, the author suffered severe post-traumatic stress disorder but recovered enough, with medical help, to be able to get a job and work in a clinical laboratory. There she met her future husband, who taught her patiently how to enjoy life. They were married for sixty blissful and enchanted years, full of love, rewarding work, and adventure.

She is now alone, sad, and lost, begging to be forgiven for all the things she did not do for him and all the loving things he did for her she took for granted.